AN EVIL PLOT

This is Lord Business. Together with his army of robot cops he rules the city of Bricksburg, making everyone follow his instructions. But there is one thing he is afraid of: the Special. A prophecy says that this person—the Special—is the only one who can find the Piece of Resistance and defeat Lord Business. Fill in the missing pieces of the picture below with the correct stickers.

One day a talented lass or fellow,
a Special One with face of yellow,
will make the Piece of Resistance found
from its hiding refuge underground.
And with a noble army at the helm,
this MasterBuilder will thwart the Kragle and save the realm,
and be the greatest, most interesting, most important person of all times.
All this is true because it rhymes.

FOLLOWING THE RULES

Just like every citizen of Bricksburg, Emmet does his morning routine according to the instructions. He loves following the rules, because that way, he's always sure to be normal, be happy, and fit in! Look at the pictures of Emmet getting ready and use your stickers, numbered 1 through 4, to put the images in order according to the instructions.

PIECE OF RESISTANCE

One day, Emmet fell into a giant hole at the construction site where he worked. At the bottom, he found something very strange: a glowing, red object called the Piece of Resistance. And it got stuck to his back! Try to find the Piece of Resistance among the scattered bricks below. Once you've found it, place the correct sticker of Emmet in the space provided.

WYLDSTYLE

Emmet was captured by Lord Business's police officers. But just in time, he was saved by a mysterious girl named Wyldstyle. Now they both have to run from the robot cops! Help Wyldstyle finish quickbuilding her motorcycle below by completing it with the correct stickers.

QUICK ESCAPE

During their escape, Wyldstyle told Emmet that there are other realms in the universe besides Bricksburg. Complete the mazes through each of the different realms. Then use the stickers to decorate the page. The stickers represent the realm Wyldstyle took Emmet to. Circle that maze.

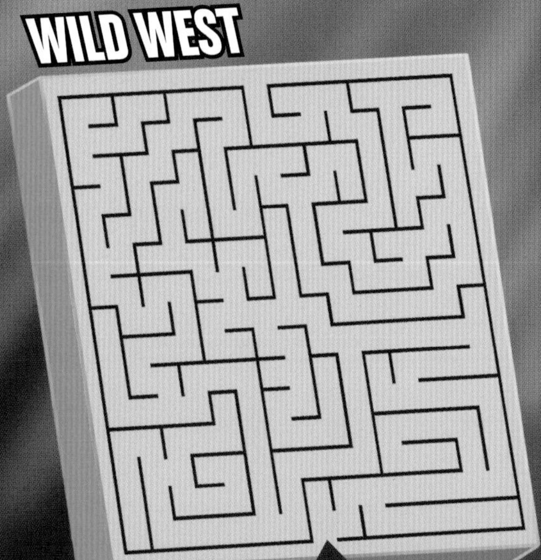

TREASURE BAY

WILD WEST

MIDDLE ZEALAND

WILD WEST

Wyldstyle and Emmet are in the Wild West looking for Vitruvius. He is the leader of the MasterBuilders and the rebellion against Lord Business. Help them find him by following the letters that spell Vitruvius's name in the puzzle below. When you succeed, place the sticker of Vitruvius at the finish point.

START

V	I	T	R	U	V	I	E	T	U	R	I	U	S	Q	A
W	G	A	O	T	B	U	F	P	N	G	K	Z	A	E	R
R	J	P	G	D	V	S	C	O	D	H	G	G	S	F	G
Y	K	O	C	A	I	H	Z	I	G	F	X	V	D	P	B
C	L	R	V	S	T	H	V	H	B	H	F	F	C	J	N
V	A	E	B	D	R	U	V	R	H	K	Y	H	V	N	P
A	D	D	N	V	T	V	I	H	X	L	H	N	I	D	O
X	U	T	M	G	A	C	U	S	E	H	I	K	V	F	I
Z	C	Y	A	D	H	B	A	V	I	T	R	U	V	G	Y
A	B	R	A	H	T	R	A	S	H	D	T	D	I	D	F
C	V	H	N	U	T	B	U	I	N	Y	I	P	U	S	I

FINISH

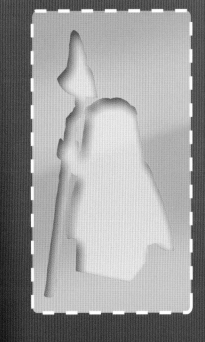

WANTED!

Lord Business's henchman, Bad Cop, has tracked Emmet to the Wild West. He has warrants with four different images of Emmet. Each row below should have the same set of four, non-repeating images. Use your stickers to fill in the missing spaces.

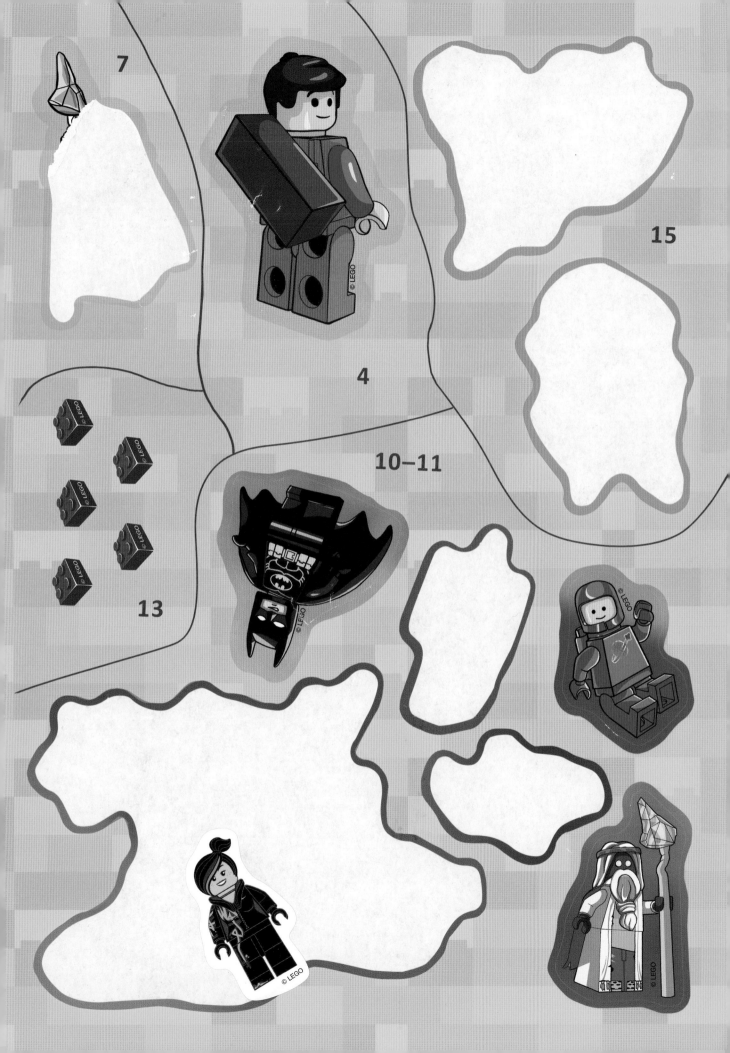

MYSTERY HERO

Bad Cop and his robo-army are chasing Emmet, Wyldstyle, and Vitruvius! Use your stickers to fill in the missing characters below. Then solve the math problems to find out who will come to their rescue. The person with the highest sum is the masked hero.

METALBEARD

7+11=

BATMAN

5+14=

GREEN NINJA

12+3=

MASTERBUILDERS

After escaping from the Wild West, Emmet met the rest of the MasterBuilders. They are heroes who are able to build anything from even the most random bricks . . . without following the instructions! Use your stickers to match the correct images of the MasterBuilders to their descriptions below.

VITRUVIUS

He is the wise leader of all the MasterBuilders, and they rely on his sage advice. Long ago, Vitruvius was blinded by Lord Business in an epic battle.

This MasterBuilder's real name is Lucy. She loves graffiti, is very brave, and is an expert at martial arts.

WYLDSTYLE

METALBEARD

This pirate is a walking battle machine. He lost his body during an attack on Lord Business's tower. But he built himself a new body . . . out of the remnants of his pirate ship.

BATMAN

This masked man of justice is the most dark, brooding, and mysterious member of the MasterBuilders. He is also Wyldstyle's boyfriend.

UNIKITTY

This half kitty, [...] es in Cloud Cuckoolan[...]m where there are no [...]s, and defini[...]

BENNY

This nice guy is a 1980-something astronaut. He really loves spaceships. As in, he's super-obsessed with them.

TOWER MAZE

The MasterBuilders want to seize Lord Business's Tower. Benny and MetalBeard are trying to get to the computer room. Lead them through the maze below by following the arrows. You can only move from one box to the next in the direction the arrows point, and be careful not to hit any robot guards! Use your brick-shaped stickers to mark their path.

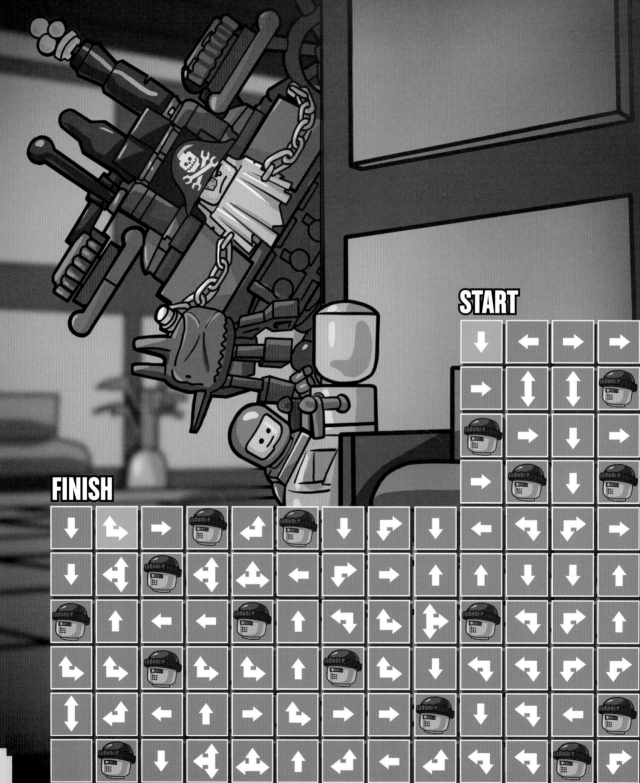

FINAL SHOWDOWN!

The MasterBuilders are launching their mission to stop Lord Business. Can you spot five differences between the two pictures below? Mark them with brick-shaped stickers.

SECRET WEAPON

Lord Business has revealed his secret weapon, and he's about to use it to glue the world together and take control of the universe! Only Emmet can stop him. Place the sticker of Emmet in the empty space and put the letters in order from biggest to smallest to read the name of Lord Business's weapon.

__ __ __ __ __ __ __

TO THE RESCUE!

The citizens of Bricksburg joined forces with the MasterBuilders to thwart Lord Business's evil plan. They threw away all their instructions and used their imaginations! Complete the picture below with stickers of the vehicles transformed into battle machines to help them save the day!

ANSWERS

Pg. 3 FOLLOWING THE RULES

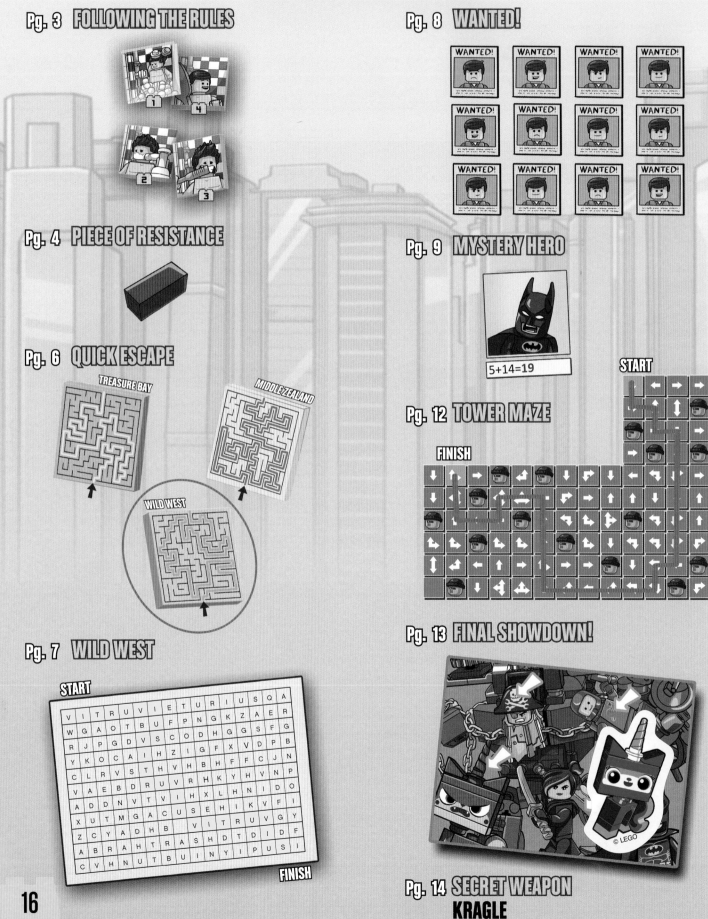

Pg. 4 PIECE OF RESISTANCE

Pg. 6 QUICK ESCAPE

TREASURE BAY

MIDDLE ZEALAND

WILD WEST

Pg. 7 WILD WEST

START

V	I	T	R	U	V	I	E	T	U	R	I	U	S	Q	A
W	G	A	O	T	B	U	F	P	N	G	K	Z	A	E	R
R	J	P	G	D	V	S	C	O	D	H	G	G	S	F	G
Y	K	O	C	A	I	H	Z	I	G	F	X	V	D	P	B
C	L	R	V	S	T	H	V	H	B	H	F	F	C	J	N
V	A	E	B	D	R	U	V	R	H	K	Y	H	V	N	P
A	D	D	N	V	T	V	I	H	X	L	H	N	I	D	O
X	U	T	M	G	A	C	U	S	E	H	I	K	V	F	I
Z	C	Y	A	D	H	B		V	I	T	R	U	V	G	Y
A	B	R	A	H	T	R	A	S	H	D	T	T	D	I	D	F
C	V	H	N	U	T	B	U	I	N	Y	I	P	U	S	I

FINISH

Pg. 8 WANTED!

Pg. 9 MYSTERY HERO

5+14=19

Pg. 12 TOWER MAZE

START

FINISH

Pg. 13 FINAL SHOWDOWN!

© LEGO

Pg. 14 SECRET WEAPON
KRAGLE

16